For Emily and
Sabrina - AC

FOR WOODROW,
VIVIANE AND
GARY - S.M.

OXFORD
UNIVERSITY PRESS

Great Clarendon Street, Oxford OX2 6DP

Oxford University Press is a department of the University of Oxford.
It furthers the University's objective of excellence in research, scholarship,
and education by publishing worldwide in

Oxford New York

Auckland Cape Town Dar es Salaam Hong Kong Karachi
Kuala Lumpur Madrid Melbourne Mexico City Nairobi
New Delhi Shanghai Taipei Toronto

With offices in

Argentina Austria Brazil Chile Czech Republic France Greece
Guatemala Hungary Italy Japan Poland Portugal Singapore
South Korea Switzerland Thailand Turkey Ukraine Vietnam

Oxford is a registered trade mark of Oxford University Press
in the UK and in certain other countries

Text copyright © Anne Cottringer 2010
Illustrations copyright © Sarah McIntyre 2010

The moral rights of the author and artist have been asserted

Database right Oxford University Press (maker)

First published 2010

British Library Cataloguing in Publication Data available

ISBN: 978-0-19-272987-3 (Hardback)

2 4 6 8 10 9 7 5 3 1

Printed in China

on of this book is a natural, recyclable product made
le forests. The manufacturing process conforms to the
al regulations of the country of origin

When Titus took the Train

WRITTEN BY ANNE COTTRINGER

ILLUSTRATED BY SARAH McINTYRE

OXFORD
UNIVERSITY PRESS

TITUS was going on a train journey. He had been on train journeys with his mum and dad, but today he was going all by himself. He was going to visit his Uncle Henry who lived **very far away.**

'The guard will keep an eye on you,' said his dad.
'Will do, Mr Templeton,' said the guard.
'Have you got your lunch?' said his mum.
'And your books? And games? We don't want
you to be bored,' said his dad.

'Yes,'
said Titus.

Soon he was listening to the
clickety - clack **clickety - clack**
of the wheels on the track.

They left the
city behind.
They
rolled
deeper into
the countryside.

Into BANDIT COUNTRY!

Suddenly from behind a bush, rushed a gang of masked men on horseback.

Titus knew they were after the gold bullion in the guard's van. The bandits leaped onto the train roof but Titus was **HOT** on their **HEELS.**

The bandits were no match for Titus.
KAPOW!
WHAM!
In a few minutes he had sent them all flying!

Back in his seat, Titus dusted himself down...

SNAP

as the train SPED into a tunnel.

The guard punched
his ticket and Titus
took out his lunch.

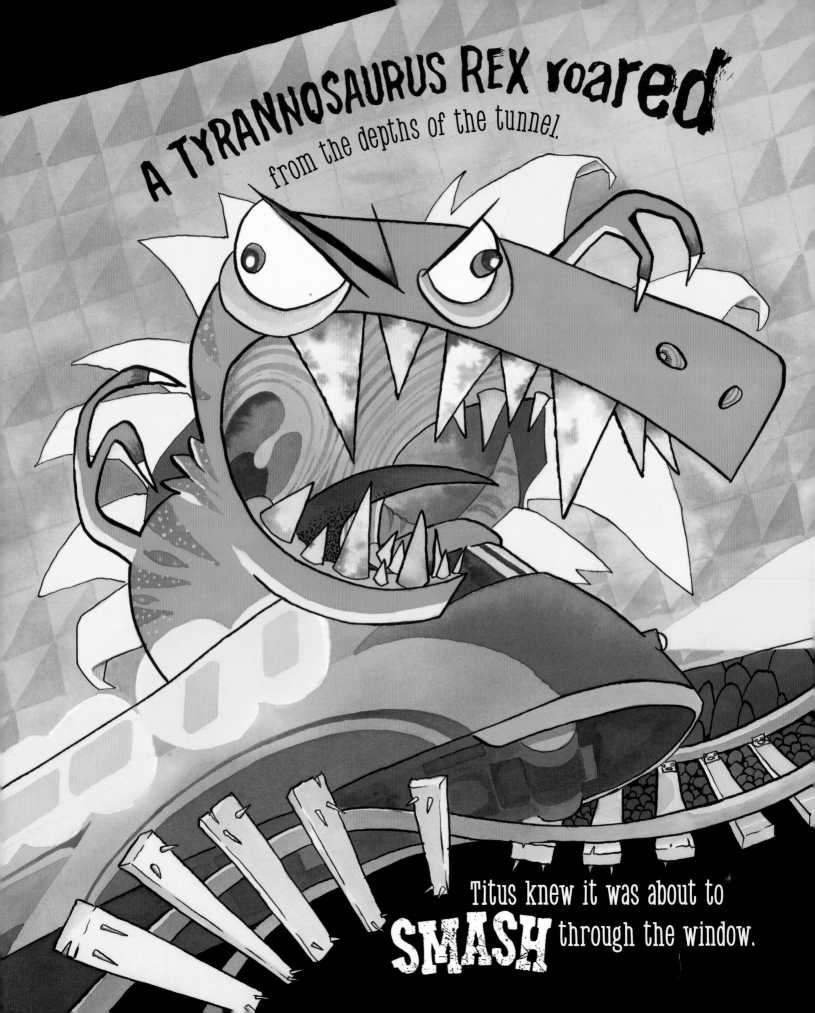

A TYRANNOSAURUS REX roared from the depths of the tunnel.

Titus knew it was about to SMASH through the window.

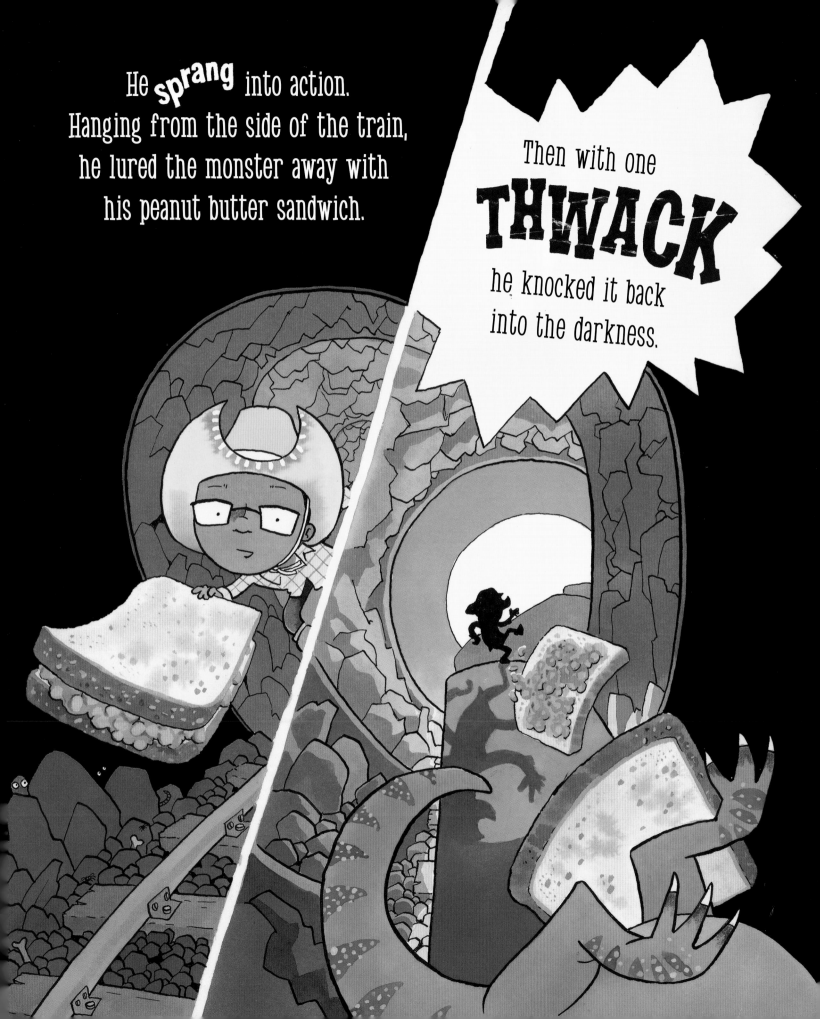

Back in ~~this~~ this seat, Titus finished what was left of his sandwich.

The train **rattled** out of the tunnel.

'Ladies and gentlemen,' said the guard, 'we are now crossing the highest and longest viaduct in the world!'

Suddenly the train **SHUDDERED to a halt.**

It had broken down.
Titus knew someone who
would help him fix it.

Before you could say Bob's your uncle, they had the train running again.

He baled out and returned with a mechanic. They **HAMMERED** and **WELDED** and **TIGHTENED** big bolts.

Back in his seat, Titus cleaned the grease off his hands.

The train wound along the edge of a river at the bottom of a steep gorge.

'Our next stop is Boulder City!' announced the guard. 'Please remember to take all your belongings with you.'

Suddenly Titus heard a loud **rumbling**.
He looked out the window. An **ENORMOUS** boulder
was **crashing** down the steep sides of the gorge.
Unless it was stopped, it was going to
SMASH into the engine!

Titus commandeered a passing canoe, shot the rapids and leaped onto the bank.

With seconds to spare, he caught the boulder and **HURLED** it into the river.

Back in his seat, Titus wiped the water from his face.

The train **climbed** up, up through the mountains. **FINALLY** it reached the top and headed down the other side.

FASTER *and* **FASTER** went the train.
Titus knew the train was out of control.
It had to be stopped!

He remembered the
BANDITS' lasso!

He **SWUNG** it over his head.

The lasso **sailed** through the air and . . .

looped over a column of rock. The train **whistle shrieked.**

The train **jerked to a halt.**

The smoke cleared.

They were
SAFE.

Uncle Henry was waiting on
the platform. 'I hope your journey
hasn't been too boring,' he said.
'It's been a bit quiet,' said the guard.

Titus just smiled
and tucked the
end of the lasso
into his pocket.